Orphan Train

VERLA KAY

illustrations *by* KEN STARK

G. P. PUTNAM'S SONS
NEW YORK

*To my marvelous editors, Susan Kochan and Nancy Paulsen, for giving
me the idea to write this story and for taking such good care of me.
Also to Charlotte Woodward for sharing her grandmother's orphan train
story, and to Pamela Ross for her "filthy feet."* —V. K.

For my wife, Chris. —K. S.

Text copyright © 2003 by Verla Kay. Illustrations copyright © 2003 by Ken Stark. All rights reserved. This book, or parts
thereof, may not be reproduced in any form without permission in writing from the publisher. G. P. Putnam's Sons,
a division of Penguin Putnam Books for Young Readers, 345 Hudson Street, New York, NY 10014. G. P. Putnam's Sons.
Reg. U.S. Pat. & Tm. Off. Published simultaneously in Canada. Manufactured in China by South China Printing Co. Ltd.
Designed by Gunta Alexander. Text set in Greco Negro. The art was done in Pebeo acrylics.

Library of Congress Cataloging-in-Publication Data ♦ Kay, Verla. Orphan train / Verla Kay ; illustrated by Ken Stark.
p. cm.   Summary: Illustrations and rhyming text tell the story of a sister and two brothers who become orphans, are taken
in, and make a journey aboard an orphan train to separate new homes. [1. Orphans—Fiction. 2. Orphan trains—Fiction.
3. Brothers and sisters—Fiction. Stories in rhyme.] I. Stark, Ken, ill. II. Title.   PZ8.3.K225 Or 2003
[E]—dc21 2001048129 ISBN 0-399-23613-9   10 9 8 7 6 5 4 3 2 1 First Impression

AUTHOR'S NOTE ♦ Between 1854 and 1929 up to 150,000 children from overcrowded East Coast cities (mainly New York and Boston) were loaded onto trains that took them westward to farming communities. While most children were placed in Midwestern states, a few went as far as California. Many of the children were orphans, but some were children of ill parents or parents too poor to take care of them any longer. The children were paraded in front of the townsfolk at specified train stations and were picked by farmers for various reasons. Some were formally adopted; most were not. Some were treated as valued members of their new families; others were taken in as unpaid laborers and were treated almost as slaves.

Babies and older boys were often the first to be chosen, as they were the most desirable. (Babies didn't have any bad habits yet, and older boys could do a lot of work on the farms.) Families were often separated, and many siblings never saw each other again or even knew what had happened to their brothers and sisters. The outrage people felt when they learned about the plight of many of these orphan-train children helped to bring about adoption reforms that made sure adoptive families were carefully screened, selected, and monitored to give children the best possible homes.

BOOTS 1443 SHOES

MILK

Horses clip-clop,
Streets unclean.
Typhoid fever,
Quarantine!

Parents coughing,
Shaking chill.
Stomachs aching,
Deathly ill.

Harold, David,
Frightened eyes.
Lucy rocking,
Lullabies.

Orphans begging
On the street.
Threadbare clothing,
Filthy feet.

Snowflakes drifting,
Winter night.
Stone-cold doorstep,
Huddle tight.

Lucy stealing,
Telling lies.
David whimpers,
Harold cries.

Children running,
Hide near bridge.
Kindly faces,
Orphanage.

CHILDREN'S AS

Months of waiting,
Orphans, clean.
Benches crowded,
Scrunched between.

Some must journey—
Just a few.
Picking children,
"You . . . you . . . you."

Railroad station,
Boisterous crowd.
Screeching engines,
Whistles, loud.

Train for orphans,
Miles of track.
Lucy wide-eyed,
Looking back.

Harold wiggles,
Swinging feet.
David sleepy,
Slumped in seat.

Station nearing,
Whistle blows.
Wiping faces,
Smoothing clothes.

Lines of orphans,
On display.
David chosen,
Pulled away.

Harold waving,
Lucy cries.
Blowing kisses,
Last good-byes.

Lurching, jerking,
Clickety-clack.
Chugging, puffing,
Down the track.

Days of travel,
Passing crops.
Railroad station,
Engine stops.

Small feet scuffle,
Shuffle, walk.
Lines of children,
Townsfolk gawk.

Standing stiffly,
Heads held high.
Harold taken,
Waves good-bye.

Lucy sniffles,
One big tear.
Wife of farmer
Pulls her near.

Ride to farmhouse,
Horse and cart.
Warm from oven,
Apple tart.

Feather pillow,
Hand-stitched quilt.
Lucy sighing,
Twinge of guilt.

"Harold ... David ...
Where'd you go?
Are you happy?
Will I know?"

Lucy milking,
Gathers oats.
Feeding chickens,
Geese, and goats.

Slowly learning,
Day by day.
Lucy giggles.
"Goat, don't play!"

Sunday service,
Wood pews, hard.
"THERE IS HAROLD!
In the yard!"

Harold shouting,
Joyous cheers.
Lucy running,
Happy tears.

Thoughts of David,
Far away.
Prayers they'll find him—
Safe—someday.